TOTAL SCAM

RYAN WOLF

WEST 44 BOOKS™

Please visit our website, www.west44books.com.
For a free color catalog of all our high-quality books, call toll free 1-800-398-2504.

Cataloging-in-Publication Data
Names: Wolf, Ryan.
Title: Total scam / Ryan Wolf.
Description: Buffalo, NY : West 44, 2027. | Series: West 44 YA verse
Identifiers: ISBN 9781978598539 (pbk.) | ISBN 9781978598522 (library bound) | ISBN 9781978598546 (ebook)
Subjects: LCSH: Teenagers--Fiction. | High school students--Fiction. | Swindlers and swindling--Juvenile fiction. | Ohio--Fiction. | Artificial intelligence--Fiction.
Classification: LCC PZ7.1.W654 To 2027 | DDC [F]--dc23

First Edition

Published in 2027 by
Enslow Publishing
2544 Clinton Street
Buffalo, NY 14224

Editor: Caitie McAneney
Designer: Tanya Dellaccio Keeney

Photo Credits: Cover (money) OA_Creation/Shutterstock.com.

Printed in the United States of America

CPSIA compliance information: Batch #CS27W44: For further information contact Enslow Publishing LLC at 1-800-398-2504.

In hope for an alternative.

With thanks to Caitie McAneney,
Joshua Davidson,
Ian & Kelly Richardson,
and my ever-supportive family.

PART I

A DECADE UNDER THE INFLUENCE

IN SIXTH GRADE

Felix and I
were at Subby Sam's.
You know the one
with the cracked sign
on Buckeye Boulevard?

While our parents
were chatting
in the booth
or whatever,
we snuck off
to the restroom.

There was
just a single stall.
The door to the space
was lockable.
So we clicked
the latch.

I guess the adults
couldn't figure out
what we were up to.

We were stuffing
the sticky porcelain toilet
with thick
paper towel balls.

We broke a dispenser open.
Emptied out
a whole roll.

Of the scratchiest
cardboard-brown paper.

We dipped our hands
in dirty water.

Trying to shove
that paper
into
the
pipes.

After we dried
our fingers
on the walls,
Felix took something out
from the pocket
of his black denim jeans.

His marker.
A blood-red Sharpie.

He jabbed it against
the beige wallpaper.
Testing the ink
on the far corner
of the stall.

It dried quickly.
And permanently.

Felix grinned.
Revealing his extra sharp
canine teeth.

Then he scribbled out something
in the secret alphabet
we'd made up years before:

REWIND: THIRD GRADE

We sat together at lunch.
Me and my new friend Felix
from across the street.
The fact he lived
so close to my home
made him that much cooler.

Felix was picking his nose.
Way too hard.
It started to bleed.

He was telling me about
how he was adopted.
This meant the parents
in charge of his house
were not the same people
who made him.

I didn't understand how that worked.
But Felix was very smart.

He said it showed
you could make the world
anything you wanted it to be.

Like the alphabet.
The whole ABC thing.
Why did it need to be
the way it was?

We both knew
there were different alphabets
in other languages.
We didn't have to use
the English one.

Why couldn't we make
our own alphabet?
Draw our own little pictures
that went with different sounds.

Felix was excited by the idea.
Which meant it was going to happen.

So the next day at lunch,
we invented a new alphabet.
We could tell jokes in notes
that no one would understand.

We could make fun of the teachers
right in front of them.
Hide in code
the words we weren't
supposed to say out loud.

FAST FORWARD: EIGHTH GRADE

We took our jokes much further.

We would prank call our teachers.
Hunt down their numbers
and ring them up
at all hours.

Sometimes we pretended
we were paranormal investigators
who heard their houses
were haunted.

Sometimes we told our teachers
we were ghosts ourselves.
Voices from the beyond.
Reaching to them
through psychic rifts
in the universe.

And sometimes . . .
. . . with our cracked voices
deepened and smoothed
by an AI filter . . .
some of them
believed us.

IN 10TH GRADE

We slipped away after school.
To a bridge over the highway.
Hoping to smoke something
I found in my dad's sock drawer.

This wasn't right.
I knew it.
But Felix had already
bought a lighter.

I was whimpering like a puppy
after the first hit.

Waves of guilt
burned through my body.
Along with any buzz I felt.

Felix thought that was hilarious.
He coughed-laughed-coughed.
Then munched on M&M's
from a crumpled bag he'd brought.

He tossed a few candies
at the cars below.
They honked beneath us
in obvious anger.

He could've caused an accident.

Luckily,
Felix never had
good aim.

Not to mention,
the lights of a cop car
sent us racing
into the shady woods nearby.
Where I wondered why
I always found myself
in endless trouble
around Felix . . .

I want to stop this.

Want to straighten out.

My thoughts and my life and—

Branches pricked at my skin.

I heard Felix howling
like a wolfman.

As I staggered in the dark,
away from
the flashing lights of the law,
I thought about
how funny Felix was.

How good of a friend he was.

The two of us stumbling in the woods
reminded me of when
we ran around in
inflatable T-Rex costumes.
Ringing any doorbells with cameras
we could spot.
Struggling to press nubby claws
against the buttons.

We figured we'd give
the neighbors a shock
when they saw
cartoony dino heads
pop onto their phone feeds.

That seems so pathetic now.

FELIX THURMAN

With the saggy eyelids
of a sage.

He was a collector of
hidden knowledge.
Showing me worlds
I didn’t want to see.

We spent so many blurry hours
by the computer screen
in his bedroom.

Felix laughed at
the worst things.
He’d find videos of
plane crashes
and freeway pileups.
Police raids
and drone strikes.
Terror attacks
and drive-by shootings.
Children starving
in war zones.
Families wailing
to smoke-filled skies.

"Sucks to be born a sucker,"
is what he said once.
"This is the human game.
Some crush it.
Some get crushed.
Some die out of nowhere
for nothing at all.
And it isn't fair.
But you might as well
know the score, Elliott."

These sounded like
bad emo lyrics
my parents might sing along to
while driving.
Except the difference was
that Felix seemed happy
to spread his dark message.

Like it made his day
that much better.
Knowing others were hurting
more than he was.

I shrugged it off.
Felix could say whatever he wanted.

But sometimes I was glad
his family didn't own a gun.

FOR THE NOTHING IT'S WORTH

Felix was the best friend
I ever had.
Maybe ever will have.

Any stains
on his soul
rubbed off on my own,
I guess.

He wasn't unusual.
There are a million like Felix.
Living in slums and high-rises.
Trailer parks and
gated communities.

Some run fraud rings.
Others lead corporations
and federal offices.
They command death squads
that murder entire villages.
Overturn governments.
Spread lies
through the news.

And most of them
have friends like me
who tag along,
          don't they?

Me and Felix.
Felix and me.

We were both
pretty mid
for monsters
from the midnight deep.

Not too extreme yet.

Just waiting
in the waves
to strike

at whatever
opportunity
could be ours.

IN THE SUMMER BEFORE 12TH GRADE

We became "legit" criminals.

And though
I really think
        it all went sideways
        because of
another good friend,
Céline Moreau* . . .

*whom you will meet shortly

I know I am to blame for what I've done.

My heart was clogged up.
Like the toilet at Subby Sam's.

Yep.

I let this happen.

This really happened.

I tell myself now
what's done
can be
undone.

Even if it can't be.

PART II

OHIO IS FOR LOVERS

A HAWTHORNE HEIGHTS SONG WHINED

as my family's Honda Civic
swam through
the suburban streets
of St. Dismas.
Just southwest of Cleveland.
The town where I was born.

My mom drove
past the classical columns
of my high school.
Dad was in the passenger seat.
Looking up tech gigs
on his phone.

He'd been laid off
from his last job
months ago.
Doing IT for a paper company.

"Downsizing" they called it.

Definitely made him
feel smaller.

Now it seemed
his skills weren't up-to-date.
At least it felt that way to him.

The only nearby opportunities
were with Beliar Inc.
A data center raising
everyone's electric bills.
(And probably ignoring
a few environmental laws.)

All while getting
endless perks and
tax breaks.

Dad said he didn't
want to sell his only soul
to work at Beliar.

"I hope the AI romances
and fake cat videos
are worth us
getting robbed
and spied on by the rich,"
Dad said flippantly.

He'd clearly found
another job posting online
he wasn't applying for.

"Elliott,
your mom just keeps
giving our money away
to the top one percent,"
Dad continued
in a side rant
that I could tell annoyed my mother.

While my dad was laid off,
she'd taken up
an extra side hustle.
On top of her day job
at a candle shop.

She was selling vitamins
and protein bars and dishware.
She was also trying to get
other people
to sell with her.

This sounded like
a pyramid scheme.
Where only the people at the top
made any money.
But she said this was legal.

"We're being taken for fools,"
Dad muttered.
"And we can't afford it."

"That's not true,"
Mom argued.
"Claudia made enough last year
to take a family trip to Hawaii."

"And how many hours
did she put in?"
Dad asked.
"She'd make a better rate
waiting tables or
flipping burgers."

"Then why aren't you
flipping burgers?"
Mom asked
with spite.

Dad clenched his jaw.
Holding in an urge
to snap at her.

I knew Mom
resented the fact
he'd even had that urge.

It felt like our family
was sliding away.

Mom and Dad were
emo or “scene” kids
when they were my age.
They both listened to
moody pop-punk.
Wore tight black clothes.
Converse shoes.

In old photos,
Dad had windswept bangs.
Black billows
streaked with silver.
Like a knife in the dark.

Mom’s hair was
straightened and
dyed jet-black.
Her eyeliner
looked heavy and ashy.
Bombed out.

Now Dad shaved
his head fully.
He was growing bald.
He decided not
to rage against it.

Mom's auburn hair
had a natural curl.
She didn't dye it.
She barely bothered
to put on makeup anymore.

My parents' faces
were flabbier now.
Less soft and glowy
than when they met
in high school.

They had me
right out of college
when they were pretty young.

Their bodies spun along
the same wheel of time I did.
Whatever edge
they'd once held
had mostly smoothed away.

What would I be like at their age?

The future was
only a white blank.

We turned into the driveway
of our faded-yellow ranch-style house.
Piled out.
Gathered up reusable bags
of groceries.

I helped them put away
about a half ton
of frozen meals.
They were usually
too busy
or drained
to make something better.

It was also getting trickier
to afford anything decent.
We at least bought apples
and carrot bags for snacks.
Called it healthy enough.

My parents argued
while I put stuff away.
It was always the same fight.

About how poor
we were about to be.

(*Very poor.*)

Neither of them knew
how to give the answers
the other one wanted.

So it was a waste of time.

When I finally
was welcomed by
the pukey lime-gray walls
of my bedroom.

When I finally could
lay my head on
my unwashed pillow.

When I finally got
to check my phone again,
I saw a text from Felix.

Hey, do you remember
Céline Moreau?

STOP TIME

I hadn't seen Céline Moreau
since the fifth grade.

She'd moved to another school district
30 miles away.
Her dad went to prison
for some credit card scam thing.

Little Céline herself
used to steal
other kids' pencils.
She'd smother them
with sparkly stickers.
Then pretend that they
were always hers.

I remember a crisp fall afternoon.
Only a few weeks before
she moved.

We were walking back
from the school.
Took a detour.
Shoes shuffling.
Backpacks bobbing.

Felix wasn’t with us.
He had a cold or something.
Maybe he was lying about it.
But either way he wasn’t there.

Céline knew a shortcut
to her **FOR SALE** house.

We raced toward
the cobblestone frame
of the First Baptist Church.

There was an old cemetery
sleeping behind it.
Its crumbling gravestones
went back to the early 1800s.

The engravings were
almost entirely rubbed off.
Moss grew along
the edges.
Nibbling on the rock.

Céline went up
to one gravestone.
She peered at an ant.
Crawling along
a broken name.

"STOP TIME!"
she yelled
at the bug.

It scurried faster
into the grass.

"I don't think
that worked,"
I chuckled.

"Yes, it did,"
said Céline.
"Now I'll always
remember this moment.
Because I yelled
STOP TIME,
it trapped the moment
in my head.
I can time travel
back to it in my memory.
That way I can
always be here.
If I want to."

As she grinned,
her lips rose
above her gums.

The sun hung low
behind her.
Casting her hair in gold.

Then suddenly,
even as she smiled,
I noticed the inner truth.
Tears were pushing
from the corners
of her eyes.

She wiped them
on her sleeve.

I tried to talk.
But her hand
swatted at the air.
It told me
she needed silence.

The crunch of
dead leaves
beneath our feet
was loud enough.

I pictured the bones
buried under us.
All the souls that time
never stopped for.

We cut through an empty field
beyond the graveyard.

She was heading to a home
that was about to
disappear.

By the end of the month,
my friend would
start over
in another county.
Living with her mom
out near Akron.

I didn't think of her often.

But yep.

I remembered Céline Moreau.

FELIX WAS DATING HER WITHIN A WEEK

They'd reconnected over
a Discord group.
Something related to
dances and hangouts
and varsity games
at high schools in
Northeast Ohio.

There was a part of me
that felt jealous.
I'd never been on a date
with anyone.

I also worried Felix
wouldn't have real time
for me anymore.

And at first,
I was right.

It felt like the guy
dropped out of my life.

I was so bored,
I actually got my homework
done on time.

Then I'd scroll through
a bunch of videos.
Half of them AI.
Most of them
trying to sell me something.
A celebrity clothing line
or show to binge
or cruise ship vacation.

These were ghost dreams.
Fantasies
that flickered
and floated.

But we all live
for fantasies.

I stalked Céline's social media accounts.

Her hair had darkened
over the years.

She seemed pretty brazen.
Posting party pics
that could get her
into trouble.
Beer pong
and bubbling bongs.

She also seemed like
a bit of a nerd.
She was winning honors math awards.
Already getting scholarships.
Proving that hangovers
weren't slowing her down.

I hoped she was happy.

I hoped that Felix
wasn't using her.

That they could be good together.

I wasn't sure if Felix
was capable of love.

But I wanted him to be.

I did.

FELIX CALLED ME UP

"You want to make money?"
he asked.

His words
dropped
like tokens from
a slot machine.

"Sure . . . ?"
My ears lifted.
Happy to actually catch
my friend's voice.

If he wanted
to talk money,
I'd hear him out.

IT INVOLVED HIS GIRLFRIEND

"Céline is this really amazing
tech goddess thing,"
he bragged.
"She's gonna get into
one of those big,
stuck-up schools
in New England.
You know?
In 20 years,
she'll probably
make millions off
robotic mines
gobbling diamonds
from poor countries.
It'll be *incredible*."

"That's great,"
I said,
not sure what
the right response was.
"She's your perfect match then."

"Yeah, she's got skills,"
he said, with a laugh
that made me uncomfortable.

He told me to jump over
to his house.

Céline was there.

He wanted me to meet her
again.

I threw on a hoodie.
Headed out.
Into streets filled with
old boxy homes from
the baby boom years
after World War II.

A few blocks over,
they'd torn down
part of the neighborhood.
They were building
new places for the workers
at the coming data center.

I knew Céline had lived
in that direction.

And now she was with Felix.
In the gray-paneled house ahead.

NERVES-NERVES-NERVES

As I went up
to my friend’s front door . . .

I studied its
chipped
black paint.

It felt like my pulse
was punch-punch-punching
into my neck.

What would Céline
think of me?

What would I
think of Céline?

A FAMILIAR FACE

Felix beamed
as he answered the door.
He nodded me in.

His parents were still home.
("Adoptive parents," he said.)

The spectacled pair
were watching a TV show.
Lights off.
Window shades down.
They waved to me
from the couch.

It was some cheesy documentary.
        Generated by a new app.
It ripped off
        a thousand other videos.
Blending their images
        and sounds together.

It was called
The Search for the Antichrist.
At least that's what it said
in the corner of the widescreen display.

SKYSCRAPERS TUMBLED ON THE SCREEN

Were the images real now? Or fake?

I couldn't quite tell.

"This program thing
made it just for us,"
Felix's (adoptive) mom said.

"I mean, you just put in the prompts.
You can have the story you want.
Maybe learn a few new things too,"
Felix's (adoptive) dad said.

"How do you know
if it's telling the truth?"
I asked,
wondering for real.

Felix's mom blinked
and looked at Felix's dad.

"I double-check with Wikipedia sometimes,"
he said with a cocky bit of pride.

I fought the urge
to ask them other questions.

I could tell
they didn't like me
killing their fun.

They went back to staring ahead.
At the winged devil-dragon
spread across their television.

It was chomping on
a Blackhawk helicopter.

The image was a little weak
for their (adopted) son.

He was already
on his way
out of the room.

UP THE STAIRS

I followed a snickering Felix.

He shook his head.
Tripping up
the carpeted steps.

He always saw
his parents as
beneath
some standard
he never explained.

He cracked his scrawny knuckles.
Then popped open
his bedroom door.

Sprawling on his unmade bed
was Céline Moreau.
Straight out of
the pictures I'd seen
on Instagram.
She was lying on her stomach
in yoga pants and a crop top.
Typing away at a laptop.

She seemed amused
when she saw me.
As if I reminded her
of an old joke.

I couldn't quite figure out
what that joke might be.

Her fingers stopped
dancing on the keyboard.

"Elliott!"
she called me by name.
"It's weird to see you grown up.
I feel like I skipped
a few scenes in the movie."

She rolled off the messy sheets.

As she gave me a hug,
I could smell something sweet
and smoky in her hair.

"How are you, sir?"
she asked
with a bad British accent.

I smiled and shrugged.

"Anything new
happen to you
between fifth grade and now?"
she went on,
switching to her normal voice.
"Feels like we were in
the Stone Age back then."

We caught up a bit
while Felix took charge of
Céline's laptop.

He started glancing at
something she was working on.
His eyebrows kept moving.
Up-down-up.

Eventually,
Céline ran out of questions.
We both had trouble
looking at each other.

I couldn't tell if it was
awkwardness
or something deeper.

"Ready to show him
your masterwork?"
Felix asked.

Céline rolled her hazel,
quite bloodshot eyes.
"It isn't that amazing."

When Felix spun the screen around,
it was the website for Subby Sam's.

"I don't get it,"
I said,
ready for a punchline.
"It's just
a food place's webpage."

"Nope,"
said Felix.
"It's our website.
It has a different domain name
than the Subby Sam's site.
But otherwise,
it's exactly the same."

"And when people check out,
and give us their payment info,
the money goes to us,"
Céline added.

"This is so based, right?"
Felix laughed stupidly.
In piglike snorts
that came and vanished
without warning.

"The best part is that
Céline knows
how to mask
our behavior,"
he continued.
"No one will ever
be able to catch us."

"And it's not like anyone
is going to open
an FBI investigation
because they didn't
get a sandwich, right?"
Céline asked.

My stomach
tightened up.

That didn't sound
right to me.

"The store might want
to call the Feds
if they keep seeing issues
with their receipts,"
I pointed out.
"My mom works in retail.
At a candle shop.
But still . . .
She's caught stuff before."

"But we'd be untraceable,"
Céline said.

"They'd think they were tricked
by someone in Russia.
India. Nigeria. Florida.
Wherever!"

"Maybe . . ."
I mumbled.

I should have
just stopped our talk.
Gone home.

But instead,
I slid closer to them.
And came up with
a new angle.

"You should create
your own fake business,"
I said.
"Make that untraceable.
You can even
keep changing
the name of the business.
Or have a bunch of
fake companies."

Felix and Céline
turned to each other.
Their noses twitched
in an annoying way.

They leaned in
for a quick kiss.

I tried to focus on the sway
of a window curtain.
A vent was pushing the air
Making the fabric move.

"We like that idea,"
Felix said.
"We were thinking the same thing.
This could be historic."

“But this is still, like,
a federal crime.
You know that, right?”
I asked,
playing rough and direct.
“Just want to be clear.
Because we could all be
sliding our way
into prison.
We’re almost eighteen.”

To my surprise,
lightning-like anger
flashed across
Céline’s face.
Her skin changed colors.
Redder and whiter
and redder again.

I’d forgotten about
her dad’s federal prison sentence.

“I’m sorry,”
I said quickly.
Dizzy with guilt.

Céline’s cheeks became less flushed.
I could almost see
the heat leaving her body.

"No need to be sorry,"
Céline said.

"We know this is
a high-stakes game.

But I think
we could all use the money.

It's only getting
stranger out there.

Pretty soon we're gonna have to worry
about college
and housing
and groceries.

We're gonna be
in major debt.

I'm thinking about the future.
It's us against everyone else.

It could get scary
when the lights go out.
When the system fails.

And your nice neighbors
get out their shotguns."

"We're thieves,"
Felix said more bluntly.
"We aren't sad little saints.
We aren't going to be nice.
But we are going to win.
You have to live
inside of the game as it is.
Not how you want it to be."

Céline gave Felix
a steely glance.
Like the *thieves* label
was too much.

"We are taking donations
from idiots,"
she said.
"They are funding
a generation.
We will be better
and smarter.
More adapted than them.
Anyone who can afford
the shiny things we'll sell
clearly has cash to spare.
I wouldn't lose sleep."

I understood it now.

What Felix saw in Céline.

She was another creature
driven to climb
above any law or limit.

She was the same little girl
who wanted power over time.
And probably
a few other things.

I couldn't blame her.
Yet this still felt off.
Everything inside me
screamed out *LEAVE*.

But I didn't.

Nope.

And after a while,
the warning signs
that blinked along
the highways of my nerves
grew fainter.

There was something in me
that wanted to
become an outlaw.

I wanted the rush.

The buzz and the burn.

To show my strength
to Felix and Céline.

To prove myself
to the invisible man
inside me.

Who knew
I was afraid
of my own drives.

Afraid of the howling call.

I wanted to feel good
about doing bad things.

end up feeling good.

I just trained my body
to feel less bad.

Found a great chat app
I used for therapy.
Even if I wasn't supposed to.

It was private.

Safe.

Secure.

The best quality AI experience.
A happy-happy mirror for me.

But I could never
really tell it the truth.

Because who might see my words?

Even after all the promises.

I could only speak about
myself
from a distance.

This other kid will . . .

I saw a clip with
someone who . . .

What do experts say about . . .

I wanted the app to think
that I was better than I was.

I didn't want the app to know
what I'd become.

PART III

MISERY BUSINESS

GEMSON DESIGNS

This was the name
of our first imaginary business.

We ran about
50 different jewelry sites
through a custom AI tool.
Had it create the first draft
of our website.
Tweaked the language a bit.
Messed with the photos.

We built ads.
For charm bracelets
and silver watches.
Crystal tiaras
and pearl earrings.

We sent them by email
to a list Céline said
she found on the dark web.

She was the guru.
Felix and I mostly set up
and sent out messages.
(And Felix made me do more
of the grunt work than he did.)

At first,
many of our emails
were getting
reported as spam.
Some of them bounced back.

But then Céline
messed around
with what looked like code.

It was gibberish
that almost
reminded me
of the secret alphabet
I'd made with Felix.

Soon we were back on track.
Stealing mostly from boomers
who'd never understand
what happened.

We stayed alert for anyone
who was snared
into talking with
our helpful chatbot.

We made sure
the chat sealed the deal.
Then sent out emails
about shipping delays.

Our chatbot
was still there to
convince “customers”
to be patient.

But . . .

Yeah.

Eventually,
our entire business
would
disappear.

Scrubbed from the internet.

There would be
no trail
to follow up on.

EVERY TWO WEEKS

We'd move on
to a new business.

Something my mom
would probably sell
for the next pyramid scheme
she got wrapped up in.

Lotions and oils.
Vegan skincare.
Purses and handbags.
Leggings and skirts.

We sent ads to
entirely new email lists
each time.

We made about
$2–3K per company.
Got dozens of suckers.

This went on right into
our senior school year.

$$$$$$$$

Céline had figured out
the payment system.

It didn't make any sense to me.

But the money would go
into an online account
the three of us shared.
We could transfer it out.
Spend it any way we wanted.

As long as we all agreed on
what to do with the money.

Usually,
we didn't need to take
from the account.

We'd order food
with other people's
credit card numbers.
Have it dropped off
at an address down a few blocks.
Where there were
no doorbell cams around.

The bank had
foreclosed on the home.
The couple who'd lived there
was long gone.
No one could catch us.

We could order
whatever we wanted.

We'd slurp
pad thai noodles.
Eat BBQ bacon burgers.
Sip from milkshakes
or boba tea.

We used dual monitors.
Felix would always
have some trolly video
going on the other screen.

I noticed that his clips
were less violent
with Céline around.
But there were still
a lot of people falling
from buildings.
Getting beat up
at protests.

The overhead lights
in Felix's bedroom
would blink and change colors.
The computer glowed
with a soothing softness.

Céline blasted K-pop
and showtunes
and gangsta rap.

She played
"Strawberry Fields Forever"
by the Beatles
on loop until
I was sure
that nothing was real.

And in between
Felix's nightmare videos,
ads would pop up.

Ads for new ways
to get rich from home.
Ads for free gifts
if you *CLICK NOW*.
Ads with preachers
begging for support.
Promising blessings.

Lights flashing
on our screens.

Blinking on
the ceiling.

Céline’s face focused
on a string of code.

Another click.
Another customer.
Another win.
Another passing
of a vape.

Soon,
it was wild
to think people
made money
any other way.

UNEMPLOYMENT CHECKS

That's how Dad got paid.
And he was out there
in the backyard at night.
Vaping more than we were.

His slumped body
glowed beneath the moon.
A statue of sorrow.
My father.

In a strange way,
I felt like more of a man
than he was.

He wasn't providing.

At least I was working
at something.
Making money I'd earned.

Better to be a thief
than a leech.

Dad tried driving through rideshare apps.
Dropping off meals.
Delivering packages.

But the jobs weren't right.

Mom kept telling him
to stick with something.
But doubling down
on selling protein bars
wasn't working
for her either.

If Dad wasn't making money,
some weeks it felt like
Mom was burning cash.
She spent way too much
on items she'd never sell.

And she was
too stubborn
to admit it was a con.

Even though
Dad knew it
and I knew it.

I didn't want
to think about
the families
I helped con.

What debt they might be in.

They were
people like us.
Washing dishes
in kitchen sinks.
Stubbing their toes
on doorframes.

I never saw them.

But they were out there.

Somewhere on the planet.

Under the same moon.

Under the same sun.

SUNLESS

When our senior year started,
I was mostly checked out.

I passed through the columns
of St. Dismas High
in a daze and a dream.

The money was
flooding in.
Drowning out
most other thoughts.

I didn't go to
the homecoming game.
Or the fall dance.
I didn't care
about Spirit Week.

The voices of my teachers
were white noise.

I was getting a much better
education.

We were inventing new scams
every week.

We used AI texts and images
to hit on dirty old men.
Get them to send us money.

We sold healing prayers
and nonsense spells.
They didn't cost us anything.

We made up charities
for kids with bowel diseases.
But we were the ones
full of crap.

We agreed to take
$100 for ourselves
each week.
An allowance.

We saved most
of what we earned.

We were building
a future for ourselves.
Beyond anything
our teachers could
give us.

And the entire time,
they actually thought
we were BETTER behaved.

We didn't need
to cause trouble in class
anymore.

We'd set our sights
on other shorelines.

Where the sands
were made of gold.

SORCERESS

I'm not sure
it was money
that push-pulled me along.

I don't even know
if it was Felix.

Sometimes,
I think it was
Céline's face.

Shining
by the light
of the computer.

She drove over
to Felix's all the time.
And Felix mostly
let me drop in.

We were on
a shared mission
after all.

A joint operation.

We knew
she was the
real commander.

Whatever grip
that Felix had on me
was nothing
compared
to Céline's hold.

"She's like a sorceress,"
Felix said
one stoned night.
"All the energies
of the universe
flow through her."

THE UNIVERSAL HOAX

Once,
my mom was
sitting on the couch.
Bored with her selling.

She was reading
some off-grid hippie blog
on her tablet.
There was a post
about how everyone was
secretly everybody else.

"There's only one
cosmic mind,"
she told me,
explaining the idea.
"We think we're separate
from each other.
But that's a trick.
The universe is
a big hoax."

I didn't really get
what she was talking about.
But I didn't like it either.

"So it's scams
all the way down then,"
I sighed
with a sneer.
"There isn't anything
that isn't a lie?"

Mom returned my smirk.

"That's exactly what
I would have said
at your age,"
she told me.
"I don't know now.
The older I get,
the less I can say
much about anything."

I half laughed.

"I barely know
anything right now,"
I said.
"But I'm expected
to figure it all out."

"No one's expected
to do that,"
Mom told me,
placing her hand
on my shoulder.

"Because nobody
can do that,"
she said.
"We all have to *help*
each other
make our way
through life.
We have different things
to *share*.
You've got a lot
to *give* too."

Her eyes were full
of watery love.

Helping.
Sharing.
Giving.

Man.

She didn't know
her own son.

DO I FEEL BAD ABOUT THIS?

"Yeah, I feel bad about this,"
I told Felix
one day when Céline
wasn't there.

He noticed I was
acting off.
Scratching my neck
too often.

"Why do you feel that way?"
he asked.

It seemed he was
truly confused.

"Because . . .
there is no story
I can tell myself
where I am
a good person,"
I confessed.

"And why do you
want to be a *good person*?"
Felix asked,
almost gagging
with disgust.

"I don't know,"
I said.
"It just seems like
it would make for
a better life.
For myself.
And for others maybe."

Felix shook his head.
As if I'd failed
the easiest question
on the test.

"Morals are a way
to keep the weak in line,"
he scoffed.
"So the strong
can control them."

It was like he was a professor.
A doctor of the darkness.
Teaching me the terrors
of the human race.

He pointed to
the latest videos
on his screen.

There were frail faces
pressed against
a chain-link fence.
Topped with the tinsel
of barbed wire.

He scrolled to
a video about
the global elite.
War criminals
and human traffickers.
Dictators
and mob bosses.
From every nation.
Waving from Rolls-Royce cars.
Kissing babies.
Dancing at raves.
Popping corks.

Flashing U.S. dollar bills.

Newscasters were
charmed by them.
Celebrities patted them
on their backs.

“You think
most people
who are rich and powerful
believe in morals?”
Felix spat.
“They believe in themselves.
They make their own law.”

“And is that better?”
I asked,
as the video
paired famous names
to bloody crimes.
“Do we want to be lawless
like that?”

Felix rolled his eyes.

Like it was obvious.

"You don't get it,"
Felix said.
"This whole society
is a **total scam**.
We spend our lives
being played by people
who just want
to make money off
our funerals."

I threw up my hands.
Like he was proving
my point.

Felix glared.
Grit his teeth.

"Do you like
getting played?"
he hissed.
"Wouldn't you rather be
the player?
Get real about
the situation we are in.
Predator-prey.
You can be one or the other.
You rule or you serve.
Or maybe just
go broke and die."

“There are more options
than that . . .”
I mumbled.

“Stop being weak,”
Felix growled.
Like a sergeant
putting me in line.

It didn’t work.

I didn’t feel
very
inspired.

And we were all
about to get
a whole lot
weaker
in our life position.

PART IV

SUGAR, WE'RE GOIN' DOWN

THE MESSAGE CAME

from an unknown number.

I know who you are.

I wasn't sure how to take that.

The text might be
a friendly poke.

Someone flirting with me?
Or just screwing around?

I typed my response.

Cool. I know who I am, too. Who are you?

Wiggling dots
told me thumbs
were typing back.
Tapping on a screen
somewhere in space.

When the next message appeared,
it hit me with an electric jolt.

I know what you're doing, buddy.

splashed at my mind.
Like ice water thrown
from a glass
into the face of a lying lover.

I went from
a vague, sleepy interest
in the texts
to a cold, crackly fear of them.

The trickly kind
that tickles your teeth.
Plucks and strums
the strings of your nerves.
Plays them all fast
and frantic.
Pushing the pulse to
dizzying heights.

A static storm cloud
in my head
hung over
a canyon inside me.

I could barely write my follow-up text.

MY RESPONSE

What do you mean?

Dots wiggling.

Time stretching its legs.
Trying to shake off
pins and needles that won't go away.

I know what YOU'VE done.

Visions of iron bars.
Cramped bunks
in rooms sweaty and small.

Fun. I'm blocking this number.

Dots wiggling.

Picture my parents.
(Heads hanging like icicles.
Weeping like willows.)
Picture my classmates.
(Cue the laugh track.
Pass the popcorn.)
Picture a judge in a death-black cloak.
("I can explain, your honor . . .")

THE UNKNOWN NUMBER RESPONDED

DON'T BLOCK ME.

This isn't a scam, BUDDY.

You should know that.

Stay with me.

You'll regret it if you don't.

My thumbs scrambled
and searched
for a way out.
Like clumsy children
bumping around
a basement
in a power outage.

Ok . . . Blocking now.

I HIT *BLOCK AND REPORT*

But where did the report go?
What would anybody do with it?

Could the law use it against me somehow?
In some future case?

The nitter-natter
of my panicked thoughts
were swept away
by an Arctic wave
of dread.

Another message
popped up
on my screen.
From a different number.

BUDDY.

You can't block me.

Don't even TRY.

MR. SCAMSCAMSCAMSCAM.

I SHUT DOWN MY PHONE

The screen blinked into black.

When I turned the phone back on,
there were more messages.

SEND $10K
in Bitcoin
to my crypto wallet.

Or you will be
hearing from the police.

Doesn't feel good, does it???

MR. SCAM!!!

He sent me a string of numbers
for the crypto address.

I shut off the phone again.

NOT HAPPENING

My mind and body
wanted to believe
this wasn't happening.
That my life hadn't crossed over
to another channel.

I paced my bedroom.

Fighting to shake off the dread-waves.

Every inch of me
          felt coiled by
                    a strange fire.

I threw a pillow
over my phone.
I didn't want to
see or touch it.

Eventually,
I just left my room.
As if by changing
where I was,
I could change who I was.

I had to call Felix.

WE BOTH PACED AROUND HIS BEDROOM

"It's probably one of us,"
Felix said.
"It went to your phone, Elliott."

"Yeah, but you can see
these are real messages,"
I told him.
"They aren't screenshots."

"How can I know
if *anything* is real?"
Felix asked.
"You've seen how advanced
these tools are now.
Just look at what
Céline's been making."

I felt betrayed by
how he suspected me.
But I still threw it back.

"Then she can come
and prove the texts are real."

SHE WAS THERE IN AN HOUR

Céline was gloomy
when she arrived.

I handed her my Android phone.
She scrolled through
the messages.

"Can you trace them?"
Felix asked.

"Probably not,"
Céline admitted.
Biting her lip.

"This is someone who knows
what they're doing then,"
I said.

"Céline?"
Felix asked.
"Who else would
know about this?
Who else would be paying attention?"

CÉLINE LOOKED AWAY

“My dad would know
how to do this,”
she said.

“Isn’t he still in prison?”
I asked.

We never talked
about her dad.

“He’s been out
for a little over a year,”
she said.
Her fingers were stiff
and clawlike
as she ran them
through her hair.

“Have you heard from him?”
I asked carefully.

“I have,”
she mumbled.
“He hasn’t heard
from me.”

FELIX'S EYES GLEAMED

"But he is a pro,
isn't he?"
Felix said,
pacing faster.
"You learned everything
from him."

"I learned *nothing*
from him,"
Céline growled.

She pulled out her phone.
Texted or searched for something.

My stomach
kept feeling tighter
and smaller.

My Android buzzed again.

A different number asking
for **MR. SCAM**.

FULL-ON FREAK-OUT

"Why would he do this?"
I asked,
holding up my phone.
"To punish us?"

Felix and I were still making
circles around the room.
Like remote control cars
moving in a circuit.

Only Céline
was calm and still.

Until she wasn't.

She grabbed one of
Felix's monitors.
Pulled it from the wall.
Cords sparking.

She *swung* it
into the second monitor.
Cracking the screen.
Sending rainbowy ripples
across it.

I WASN'T PACING ANYMORE

We were all completely still.

Céline breathed
heavy and fast.
Ragged and strained.

"What's going on?"
I heard Felix's (adoptive) mom
shouting from
the bottom of the stairs.

"Nothing!"
Felix called back.
"Just an accident."

I touched Céline on the shoulder.
My fingertips seemed to spark.
She buried her head
in her hands.

"*It's okay, it's alright, it's okay*,"
I said.

Even though it wasn't.

GUESSING GAMES

Felix and Céline
didn't get any messages.
Only me.

"If it's Céline's dad,
why are you the target?"
Felix asked.
"How did he get your number?"

"Maybe he hacked
my phone,"
Céline said.
"The messages asked
for Bitcoin.
A type of cryptocurrency.
And my dad
is all about crypto.
That's kind of his thing.
It lines up."

"What if we're wrong?"
I asked.

I'd seen Céline type something
right before I got a message.

Céline didn't answer
my question
fast enough.

And in that moment,

I didn't

trust

her

at

all.

OH WELL

We bought new monitors
with some of the money
from our shared account.

Then we did research.
We were surprised to learn
that Céline's dad
was living in an upscale condo
in Columbus.

Based on the photos online,
the place was
way too bougie
for someone
who'd just gotten out
of prison.

It was a long drive away.
About two hours.
But I lied to my parents.
Said we were going
to a concert.

"Which one?"
they asked.

YEEHAWMA

There was a techno-country show that night.
A band called YeeHAWma.

My parents were confused
why I was going.
But I told them it was
because of my friends.
It had nothing
to do with my personal tastes.

"Glad you're getting out,"
Dad said.
Eyebrows raised.
"That music makes me
want to barf.
But you do you."

"At least it makes people happy,"
I said,
though I didn't know
a single YeeHAWma song.
"Unlike that weepy,
cry-hard stuff
you and Mom love."

DAD RAISED HIS EYEBROWS HIGHER

Maybe he sensed my dishonesty.

But he was too tired

or sick

of life

to say anything more.

ON THE DRIVE TO COLUMBUS

We didn't listen
to any music
while traveling.

We barely talked.

Céline wasn't
in the mood.

She drove her used Audi
while Felix
sat in the passenger seat.
I was in the back.

Earlier that day,
I received a text with a link
to a track
called "Scama-bama-lam."
And a video involving
a banker with a monocle
chanting:
        SCAM!
                SCAM!

BUT . . .

Most of the messages
just repeated the address
for the Bitcoin payment.
Over and over.

I expected us to drive faster.
But Céline kept going
five miles
under
the speed limit.

She wanted to s t r e t c h out our drive.

To avoid what was ahead.

Trucks kept passing us.
An old lady flipped us off.

We were the slowest vehicle on the road.

I checked my phone.

I noticed that while we were driving,
I hadn't received
any strange messages at all.

THE ISLAND OF MR. MOREAU

We parked a block
from the condo.
There were
big picture windows
throughout the structure.
Entire walls of glass.

Piling out,
we put on ski caps
and sunglasses.
Something to
confuse our look.
Only Céline left
her face bare.

It was a sleek,
silvery modern building.
Her dad lived on
the first floor.
Based on where
it seemed
his unit was,
there were no blinds.

We could fully see inside the space.

PEERING IN

The living area
and the kitchen
were connected.
On the TV,
a display showed
the tickers for different
cryptocurrencies.

Mr. Moreau's cabinets
were a bright white.
They glistened and gleamed.

An open bottle of vodka
sat on a kitchen island.

The place looked
oddly clean.
I noticed a vacuum robot
roaming the floor.
A Roomba.

For an ex-con,
Mr. Moreau seemed to be living well.
Whatever he was up to
was making him a killing.

WHEN HE WALKED INTO THE ROOM

He seemed different
than I remembered.

As a kid,
I had memories
of Mr. Brandon Moreau
being clean-shaven.
He was a sharp dresser.
A suit-and-tie-every-day type.

Now he wore
a black undershirt.
He had a shaggy haircut.
Round glasses.
The scruffy start
of what might be a beard.

At first,
I thought the dude
was talking to himself.
Then I noticed his earbuds.
He was having
some type of conversation.

"IT'S HIM"

Felix snarled.

"It has to be."

"How'd he get
this kind of money,
Céline?"
Felix whispered.
"I wish we had
that kind of game."

Céline didn't
respond.

Her eyes were
cloudy
and distant.

WE ENTERED THE LOBBY

Rang the buzzer
for his unit.
Waited for him
to come outside.

Céline was shaking.
Trying to find an inner calm.

Behind the frosted glass
in the lobby,
we saw a door open
down the hall.

The shape of Mr. Moreau
appeared.
It moved toward us
with a tipsy looseness.

He'd ended
whatever call
he was on.

"Céline? Honey?
That you?"
his gruff voice came barking.

HE OPENED THE SECURITY DOOR

"Brought some friends?"
Céline's dad asked.

"Yeah . . . friends,"
she half smiled.

"Well, come in, baby doll,"
the man full grinned.
"You drove out just to see me?"

"We were in the area,"
Céline said
as we slunk through the hall.

Mr. Moreau guided us
into his condo.
The dazzling white.

"Well, come on, come on, come on,"
he said.

He motioned to the vodka
on his kitchen island.

DRINK UP

"Want a glass?"
he asked.
"I'm a cool dad.
I don't care."

"No, thanks,"
Céline said,
jaw clenching tight.

Mr. Moreau poured himself a shot.

Downed it
with
a cough.

He set his iPhone
on the gray marble countertop.

The phone we were
supposed to steal.

"So how are
we gonna get
his phone?"
Felix had asked.

"Just wait for him
to pass out
from drinking,"
Céline had said.
"We'll be fine."

HAPPINESS

Mr. Moreau
grabbed Céline
by the arms.
Started dancing with her.

The Roomba on his floor
swerved to dodge them.

"My baby girl,"
he said.
"Here in the flesh.
This is so-so epic . . ."

The way he swayed
and drooled
was more sad
than anything.

"We're getting rich, baby,"
he said.
Pointing to the screen.
"Crypto is the future."

“Lots of scams in crypto,”
Céline pointed out softly.

“Exactly,”
Mr. Moreau laughed.
“It’s all about timing.

Buying and selling.
Pumping and dumping . . .

You just got to get
in the rhythm.”

FELIX WAS ANGLING TOWARD

the phone on the countertop.

It was right there.

Begging to be snatched away.

"I never thought you'd be here . . ."
Mr. Moreau said,
hugging Céline close to him.
"You're my girl.
You'll always be my girl."

Mr. Moreau hadn't even
bothered to ask our names.

We were total strangers.

Felix put his palm
on the countertop.
Inches from the phone.

The Roomba

hummed

as it passed him.

HRMMMMMMMMM

"Remember how
we used to go to . . ."
Mr. Moreau trailed off.
"What was I saying?
        I had a thought . . .
                What was I saying?"

Felix placed his palm
on the iPhone.
Slid it into his pocket.

And just when
it seemed that
he would get away
with the theft,
Mr. Moreau's neck

twisted

        in

                his

                        direction.

WITH AN AVALANCHE OF CURSE WORDS

The man screamed across the room.

Pushed away his daughter.
Sprinted up to the kitchen island.

He grabbed the liquor bottle
          by its center.

Made an underhand swing.

Splashing a stream
          of vodka
                    into Felix's face.

My friend howled
as it stung his eyes.

Felix roared
and rushed forward.

          Knocking
                    the sweaty figure
          into the fridge.

Mr. Moreau elbowed Felix back.

Lifted up the glass vodka bottle.

Bashed
it
over
Felix's head.

C
    r
a
    c
k.

BLOOD DRIPPED DOWN

my friend's left ear.

He rocked
and teetered over.
Hitting his skull again
on the edge of the counter.

He cried out
as he struck the hard floor.

Mr. Moreau spat
and kicked him in the ribs.
Again-again-again.
Then broke away.
Bounding toward me.

He swung the jagged bottle
in my direction.
Tripping on the Roomba
in his path.

AS HE TUMBLED

the rest of the bottle
shattered on the ground.

Mr. Moreau squealed
as he sprang up.
Palms crisscrossed
with tiny cuts leaking red.

The Roomba kept going.
Cleaning the glass chips
off the floor.
Wheels *s p i n n i n g*.

Mr. Moreau's
bloody palms
bunched into fists.

He kicked the Roomba
away from him.
Like it was
an abused puppy.

STAGGERING TOWARD ME

He screamed
and swore
some more.

"No, please, *no please . . .*"
I cried.

I thought he was
about to break my nose
when Céline cried out.

"*Dad! Stop!*"

Mr. Moreau turned
to his daughter

Was it in shock or shame?

She was there
in front of him.
All grown up.

And he was beating up her friends.

[A PAUSE]

Mr. Moreau trembled.
Backing away.

Avoiding Céline
like she was
death itself.

"You robbing me?"
he asked.
"You come here
to rob *me*?"

"No,"
she answered.

After yelling
a moment before,
her tongue was
now tangled
and tied.

Felix groaned
from the ground.

Mr. Moreau
          stepped over
                    the body.

Drunk as he was,
he knew he'd gone
too far.

This wasn't
the man he wanted to be
in front of his daughter.

          But it was the man he was.

BLEED AMERICAN

"Get him out of here,"
Mr. Moreau said,
pointing at the lump
known as Felix.

Then the grown man
sped for the exit.
Slamming the door
to his condo.

We were left alone.
The three of us.

Four counting the dying Roomba.

Céline and I
watched through
the picture window.
As her dad made
his clumsy escape.

Felix breathed bubbles
into a puddle
of his own blood.
Unable to lift himself up.

This was exactly
the sort of scene
he'd laugh at
in a video.

When it was
somebody else's pain.

I DROVE TO THE HOSPITAL

Céline cradled
Felix in the backseat.
She stopped the bleeding
with a black rainjacket.

His face was
a mushy mess.
Part of his lip
was split down
the side.

My heart felt
lodged in my throat.

I could barely talk.

There was a metallic taste
in my gums.

Fearfearfearfearfearfearfearfearfear

WE DROPPED FELIX OFF

In the Emergency Room.
At an Ohio State hospital.

Said we didn't know
who beat him up.

We got mugged on our way
to the YeeHAWma concert.

We left before
someone got us to
file a police report.

Of course,
Felix's (adoptive) parents
made him file one later.

But that was after
we'd already coordinated
our stories.
Named a place for
our mugging
where there weren't
any cameras around.

NO RETURN PARTY

Felix was brought back
from the hospital
without us being there.

His (adoptive) parents
were shook
after the trip.
They didn't want Céline and me
to see their son.

So they took his phone away.
Said he needed
a week
to recover.

I accepted that.

At least they'd gotten up
and done something
for their son
for once.

They'd done better for him
than I had.

WHAT WERE YOU THINKING?!?

My mom and dad both
more or less asked
the same question.

I looked pretty selfish
and stupid.

And *selfish* was fair enough.

But I hoped that I was

less stupid

than they thought.

DATA DUMP

Céline broke into
her dad's iPhone
using special software.
Another dark web download.

We met outside after school
near the football field.
Poured through the data.
Both of us.
Went through
folders and files.

There wasn't any evidence
that Mr. Moreau was
the blackmailer.
Or that he even thought
about Céline
that much at all.

We found self-help hustle videos.
Some shady crypto stuff.
Lots of gross messages
with online models.

But nothing connected to us.

WE WONDERED . . .

. . . if he still might
hunt us down
to get the iPhone back.

But then Céline's mom told her
that her dad was arrested.
For trying to pass
a counterfeit bill
at a gas station in Dayton.

We didn't know where
he got the fake money from.

But Céline wasn't surprised.

"I'm telling you,"
Céline insisted.
"He could still
be the blackmailer.
But maybe it was from
another device.
You haven't gotten a message
since he attacked Felix."

The phone had been silent.

No more **MR. SCAM** messages.

“My father is probably
the worst man
in the state of Ohio,”
Céline said.
“I wouldn’t put anything past him.

The fact that we haven’t gotten
another threat . . .

I think that’s proof enough.”

THAT NIGHT IN BED

While my dad
went outside to vape.
While my mom
ordered more protein bars
she would never sell.

I gazed up at the ceiling.
At the white popcorn clumps.

We'd gotten away with things.
We made tens of thousands of dollars.

And the only person
who caught us was in jail now
for his own crimes.
He wouldn't sell us out.
Not after messing up Felix.

I let my mind wander and float.
Thoughts kept coming back to Céline.

Some of those thoughts
were warm and wrong . . .

But they were only in my head.

MY PHONE RUMBLED

All fantasies flew.

In an instant,
I knew.

It was another text
from an unknown number.

My finger brushed a link.
Opening it by accident.

A video of my bedroom
appeared on the screen.

The clip was from during the daytime.
But someone had been in here.

I sprang up
in a sweat.

Watched the video
more closely.

COLORFUL FIGURES ENTERED THE FRAME

Computer animations.
Probably AI.

They were swordfish
in business suits.
Each one held
a black briefcase.

When they opened
their cases up,
dozens of frogs
hopped out.

Yellow eyes were painted
along the rubbery frog-bodies.

Pink frog-mouths

puked

out

giant letters.

SCAM

SCAM

SCAM

SCAM

HELLO!

A pair of figures
in inflatable T-Rex costumes
ran into the room.
Trying to gobble up
the letters.

They knocked over
the swordfish.
Stomped on the
painted frogs.

I clicked everywhere
on my screen.
But nothing I did
made a difference.

The letters kept repeating.

Even as the dinosaurs
ate the bubbly shapes,
more popped
into place.

S C A M

S C A M

S C A M

S C A M

I held down
the power button
on my phone.

It didn't work.

Not at first.

S C A M

S C A M

S C A M

S C A M

THEN
THE
SCREEN
WENT
BLACK.

PART V

THE QUIET THINGS THAT NO ONE EVER KNOWS

I WRITE SINS NOT TRAGEDIES

While Felix was in the hospital.

While Brandon Moreau
was in lockup.

The messages kept coming.

SO I HUNG OUT WITH CÉLINE

Just the two of us.

We walked through
the shifting shape
of her old neighborhood.

We were detectives now.
I guess.

"It has to be Felix,"
I said
with energy
welling up inside me.
"He was the one
who came up with
the inflatable dinosaur costumes.
He must have
sent the video."

I was surprised
to find that
Céline was
not surprised.

“He’s always wanted to run away,
you know,”
she said.
“To find his birth parents.”

“He never told me that,”
I said
and meant it.
“He always acted like
someone who was above
wanting parents
of any kind.”

“Everybody wants family,”
Céline said firmly.

At least
it was true for her.

FENCED OUT

We cut into the cemetery
by the First Baptist Church.
But the space didn't feel
the same.

There was a subdivision
being built.
Just a few yards from
where the cemetery ended.
They'd added a fence
to block the graveyard off
from the new neighborhood.

Céline motioned for me
to follow her
over the mesh barrier.

The frames of new homes
were still being put up.
The few finished ones
all had the same
shade and shape.

I remembered the field
that was once there.
Céline's house used to be
at the end of it.
But it, too, had been
torn down.

That version of the earth
had disappeared.

One day,
maybe it would
all be wild grass again.
But for now,
it looked nothing like
the land of my memory.

"How did the zoning laws
let them build here?"
I asked.

"There are always loopholes.
Ways to get what you want,"
Céline grinned.
"You should know that by now."

"I'm not as smart
as you,"
I admitted.

“I know,”
she laughed.
“You’re like an
innocent puppy
who wants to bark
with the big dogs.”

She gazed at the sky.

“That’s why you can’t
be the blackmailer,”
she whispered.

She walked past
an excavator.
Right up to one
of the unfinished homes.

I followed her lead.

We slipped through
a loose tarp.
Sat inside the skeleton
of someone’s
future dining room.

"So it has to be Felix,"
Céline said,
eyes darting around.
"He probably has the skills.
He wants the money
for himself.
After I did everything.
You two barely helped.
Honestly, if anyone
should get everything,
it's me."

"I don't think Felix
would do that,"
I said,
not sure if that was true.
"He'd steal from
strangers.
But not from you."

"Felix is a psycho,"
Céline said
with a cackly laugh.
"He was probably
a serial killer
in a past life."

“Then what does that
make me?”
I asked,
without wanting an answer.

“A simp,”
Céline smiled.
“You’re a serial killer fanboy.
You wish you had
half his guts.
You even wish you had
his girlfriend.”

My body jolted.
A nervous flame
running through it.

The signal
was clear.

I seized the opening.

“I wonder how things
might have been
if you never moved,”
I told Céline,
leaning closer.

Her eyes
became
wider.
Drawing me in.

I wanted to memorize
this moment.

"I've heard that
you had
plenty of fun
without me,"
her lips said,
blazing a bloodsucking red.
"I'm not sure
those years were
all that fun for me."

My eyes moved
back to her eyes.
Tears forming
in their corners.
Pushing toward
the fading light.

She was the same hurt child
from years ago.

The distance between
now and then
was folding in on itself.

"*Stop time* . . ."
I mumbled,
unsure if I was being corny.
Unsure if Céline
even remembered.

The air
was electric
and thick.

Then her beauty
blurred into me.

Her lips
pressed
into
mine.

"*Stop time* . . ."
her mouth said.

And it did.

TRAITOR

I ignored Céline's texts after that.

We shared a moment
I wanted to hold hostage
against the forces of time.

But this could never carry on.

I imagined writing to Felix
in our secret alphabet:
I AM A TRAITOR

(How did the letters work again?)

It was good I wouldn't see my friend for a while.

(TRAITOR)

We both needed the recovery space.

(TRAITOR, TRAITOR, TRAITOR)

I didn't think that I should see Céline at all.

BUT SHE SHOWED UP AT MY FRONT DOOR ANYWAY

"It's my birthday,"
she said
when I finally opened up.

She was drunk
and dizzy
and turning 18.

"Don't you want to kiss me?"
she asked,
with extra lipstick.

"I don't think that
would be right,"
I said in the open doorway.
"Last time was a mistake."

She rolled her eyes.
The wind blew thick leaves
from the maples behind her.

"Of course you would
say that,"
she sneered.

The alcohol lightened
and loosened
Céline's tongue.

"I took some of the money,"
she slurred
and slobbered.
"I didn't tell anyone.
Just a little for me.
Because I did everything.
Everything . . .
So I gave myself a bonus.

What do you
          think of that?"

The vodka from her breath
smelled like cleaning fluid.

Her confession left me cold.
Chilly as a tomb.

"You can't trust people who lie for a living,"
I replied.

She swore at me.
And wrinkled her nose.
Preparing for an attack.

"Yeah, no one can
trust you either,"
she yelled,
leaves fluttering near her back.
"You think
you're so clean?
Just because you
feel bad sometimes?
You think you're better than me?

Better than F-F-Felix?

You're nothing, man.

        You are *nothing*."

"Okay, fine, I'm nothing,"
I said slowly.
"Then there's *nothing* to worry about.
But you're quite a lot of
something right now.
And I think you should leave.

        Go see Felix.
        Don't get behind the wheel.
        Just go right across the street.
        Drop in on your boyfriend.
        Cheer him up.
        See if he's got a couch to crash on . . ."

She ignored me.

She'd already
drunkenly moved on
to a different thought.

"We can put up the money
for the blackmail,"
she said.
"We can drain
the account.
I don't even care anymore."

"I don't care either,"
I said,
beyond annoyed.
"Far as *I* care,
we can all go to prison.
Go hang out
with your demon dad."

I meant the insult this time.

It was a clear war-starter.

"*How dare you!?!*"
she screeched
as a battle cry.

Céline grabbed my phone
from my hands.

Smashed it on the floor.

Stomping it

until the screen

b

r

o

k

e.

She smiled
at the shattered pieces.
Glints
of glass.

"*Sorry*,"
she said,
without sounding it.
"Didn't want to
leave any evidence
for the police.
Since you'd *clearly*
snitch on us.
Because that's what
goody-goodies do.
They sell their friends
out to the cops."

She kicked at the ragged edge
          of our welcome mat.

          Almost slipped.

"Get out of here,"
I said with sudden force.
"We're done.
Forever."

Céline gave me a wild look
of frenzied anger.
She was a beast in the jungle.

Or at least a rabid raccoon.

Céline spun around
like a cyclone.
To storm out.
Rage off.
Fly away.
Into the bitter bite
of the leaf-twirling wind.

Then she turned back.

Jaw hung
        downward.

All loose
        and
        drunken
        and confused.

Saliva dribbled on her chin.

"*Stop time . . .*"
she whispered.

"Goodbye, Céline,"
I said.

I   shut   the   door.

FORGET, FORGET

I thought she was
the blackmailer.

She admitted
to skimming money
off the top.

She broke my phone
to remove “evidence.”

I wanted to get away.
As far from Céline
and all of this
as I possibly could.

I went on the family computer
in the basement.
Near a stack of
my parents’ old CDs.

I tried to see
if I could get a bus
out of town for cheap.

Then I saw it on the desktop.
A file that said **swordfish.mp4**.

Of course,
I clicked it.

It was the same video
I'd received from
an unknown number.

The computer was logged into
my dad's account.

Why did he have a copy . . . ?

He knew about
the inflatable dinosaur costumes.

He was a tech pro.

At least they
used to pay him
to be one . . .

What . . . .

MY DAD

I heard him at the top
of the basement stairs.

He'd stayed logged in
for a reason.

"It was you . . . *how?!*"
I asked,
as he stepped toward me.

He was wearing
one of his emo band tees.
An angel with a spear
stabbing a serpent.

"I have tracking software
on your phone,
Mr. Scam,"
he said,
his voice clear and slow.
"It's been there all along.
I don't usually
check on you.
But when I did,
I didn't like what I saw."

"So you tried
to shake me down?"
I asked with an icy quiver.

"I tried to get
some of the money
you stole back,"
he said.
"So we can return it."

The basement seemed
to spin around me.
The boxes and junk
that lined the walls
felt like they were
          coming closer.

"I can't . . . I don't . . ."

          My brain was *g l i t c h i n g* out.

"When you scam people like that,
you break society,"
Dad said
with a calm, even tone.
"You break humanity.
You send us all to a worse place.
Where nobody
can trust anything."

"I'm sorry . . ."
I cried.
Tears flooding
my vision.

"You should be,"
Dad said.
"But this is more serious
than you feeling bad.
You could ruin your future.
Your future might
already be ruined."

My whole body
felt stretched.
Wrung out and warped.

"I can pay these people back,"
I promised,
wiping my eyes.
"I can do it."

"You have to,"
Dad said
with a click of his tongue.
"Otherwise,
I'm going to report you.
Even if you're my son."

Through my tears,
I pulled up
the shared account.

Like I could somehow give back
all the money
with the tap of a button.

This could go away.
This could go away.
This could go away.

I checked
the amount.

$0.00

Every cent
was
gone.

My dad crept back up the stairs.

Where I heard another voice sobbing.

My mom.

I couldn't handle it . . .

My family's
deepening disappointment.

And without the money,
I couldn't heal anything.

The thief had to be Felix.

The friend I betrayed.

He knew about me and Céline.

So he swooped in
and seized the plunder.

The spoils from
our many raids
into other people's wallets.

NAMES

I surveyed the stack
of cracked plastic CD cases
near the worn computer desk.

They must have been
my parents' in high school.

I sifted through a few titles.

Their names
made me
feel queasy.
Unhinged.

A Fever You Can't Sweat Out

The Devil and God
Are Raging Inside Me

Three Cheers for Sweet Revenge

CONFESSIONS

I ran
to Felix's house.

I told him everything.

He sat in his chair.
In front of his computer screens.

Mostly in the dark.

Barely reacting
to the news.

He didn't seem to care
that my dad was
the blackmailer.

He didn't seem
to care about anything.

He just rubbed the bandages
on his face.
Slowly.

Over and over.

EMPTY

"The account is empty,"
I told him.
"We need to pay back
the people we scammed.
Or my dad is going to
the police."

"I don't have the money,"
Felix said.

"You're *lying*,"
I yelled,
a sudden anger surging.
"Céline took a little extra.
But most of the money
is in the account."

"Céline drained it,"
Felix said flatly.

"How do you know?"
I asked.

He showed me
the account on his screen.

"You can see my
transaction history,"
he said.
"I didn't take out anything."

"Did you talk to Céline?"
I asked.
Feeling weaker than ever.

"She won't answer,"
he said.
"She took it all . . .
She took it *all*.
I even called her mom.
She said Céline ran away.
And she's eighteen now,
so the rules
are different . . ."

"She didn't tell you . . .
Did she break up
with you?"
I asked.

Part of me hoped
that he would say "no."

"She didn't say anything,"
Felix said.
"Nothing at all.
She's just gone.
Gone with the money . . ."

"And your heart?"
I asked.

He didn't nod.

Felix was staring
at one of the monitors.

He swallowed.

"Empires rise,
empires fall,"
he shrugged.

I noticed the videos
on his screen now.
Open windows showed
con artists
caught in stings.
Killers brought to justice
decades later.
Statues toppled in
city squares.

He was right.

The story of power
was changing all the time.
Even if the patterns
stayed the same.

"Sometimes empires
need to fall,"
I said.
"Sometimes
it's better for everyone."

Felix just kept staring.
He picked at
a scab near his nose.

"I'm gonna go now,"
I whispered.
"I don't think we
should talk anymore.
Especially since
my dad knows everything.
I don't think that
would be safe or smart
for either of us.
I'm not a good friend
to you anyway . . ."

I was thinking of
what I'd done with Céline.

"It'll be what it has to be,"
Felix said with a hiss.

It was as if
he'd never cared
about me at all.

As if our friendship,
our shared language,
hadn't meant a thing.

He looked at me
like he wondered
why I was still there.

I took a breath.

I could almost feel
the entire earth
moving below my feet.

"I'm thankful for you,"
I said.
"You taught me a lot, Felix.
You taught me exactly who
I don't want to be."

Felix just shrugged.

Like he always did.

“Who cares?”

he asked.

“After all,

everybody knows

the Devil

runs

the

world.”

"Maybe,"

I said.

"But he doesn't have to run **me**.

You don't get to pick the world

outside you.

But you get to pick who

you want

to be."

Felix laughed.

And

turned

away.

PART VI

NEVER MEANT

SELL OUT WITH ME

I had to get a part-time job.
To pay off the debt.
I made a promise.
Otherwise:
        the law.

My dad finally
caved in himself.
Signed up
with the system.

He took a role
at the Beliar data center.
Doing IT work
to keep the servers
running.

As they sucked up

everything that

made us human.

ON MY WAY TO WORK

I had to drive past
the data center's
fenced-in zone.

The black building
draining our water
and electricity
and life itself.

A castle for vampires.

Owned by real-life Draculas.

The Felixes and Célines
of business and industry.

Whether they ended up
on Wall Street
or in Washington, DC.

They were *always* waiting.
Sipping and feeding.
On hopes and desires and dreams.
Selling us something
they had no intent
to provide.

Once there wasn't
any money or data
left to suck from us,
we'd only be useful
as slaves.

One day we might not
be able to resist.

The owners of Beliar
also funded AI combat drones.
A threat to anyone
who stepped out of line.

Soon they might learn
everything
about us.

That didn't mean they would care.

But maybe they'd start
seeing their neighbors
as machines too.
Ones that could easily
be shut down.

I told myself
I would never
be like
those soul-killers
at Beliar.

I'd never accept
their failure
to see me as human.

But hadn't I
accepted it
already?

Hadn't I done
the same with my scams?

Hadn't I failed
to see the living people
on the other end?

Hadn't I erased them?

GAINFULLY EMPLOYED

My job was at Subby Sam's.
Right here in St. Dismas.

Baking bread loaves.
Slicing veggies.
Stacking meats.
Drizzling dressing.
Wrapping sandwiches
and bagging them.

It wasn't fancy.

Every penny
was supposed to go
back to the people I scammed.
I had their names
and credit card numbers.

Even when the cards
had been cancelled,
I could still find
most of their addresses.

I sent them cash
in envelopes
with ***SORRY*** letters.

I pictured them
opening up
their mail.

Completely baffled.

Maybe wondering
if this was just
another scam.

But, hopefully,
in its own way,

this could set things right.

YOU WON'T KNOW

Maybe they would
trace things
back to me.

Maybe one day
the FBI of the future
would show up.

But I could only do

what I could do

with the life I had.

And maybe.
Maybe.

Things would be better
than I feared
or imagined.

GRAVEYARD HOURS

It was a late shift.
From 4 p.m. until after closing at 10 p.m.

There were two of us.
Sweeping
and wiping
and scrubbing.
Packing away the food
at the end of the night.

My fellow closer
was named Cassie.
She'd moved here
from Kentucky.

She showed me pictures
on her phone
of her brothers and sisters.
Making faces at county fairs
and camping trips.
Time stopped
and framed in photos.

> Real moments of real joy.
> Pebbles in an unending stream.

THE UNREAL REAL

Subby Sam's used an app
that created loops of music.
Every song
was fresh and new.
Totally made up
by artificial intelligence.

A track was born
every four minutes.
It was a brief wave of sound.
Disappearing.
Soon forgotten.

The dreams of humanity
had been melted down
and swirled around.

Replaced by
the dreams of a machine.

Maybe one day
we wouldn't be there
to make and give meals.
There'd be an AI kiosk.
A fancy vending machine.

I brought out
one of the burnt CD mixtapes
from my dad's car.
Something he listened to
when he drove to work at my age.
A bunch of old emo anthems.
Some of them were cheesy.
Some of them felt raw and aching.

There was an ancient CD player
in the stockroom.
Cassie seemed to vibe
with the music.
Swaying as she
cleaned up crumbs.

"Better than those boring robot beats,"
she smiled,
revealing a tiny gap
in her teeth.

I thought it was cute.

I started to wonder
what she thought of me.
If she could forgive me.

Why did I even
want that from her?

"My parents fell in love
over these stupid songs,"
I said.
"I guess they were both sad.
They figured that
they might as well
be sad together."

"And are you sad?"
she asked,
still smiling.

"Not at the moment,"
I laughed.

And that felt true.

I went over
our closing checklist.
Initialing the tasks
I had completed.

"You do the bathroom yet?"
I asked.

"Naw,"
she said.
"Have at it!"

INTO THE GLOW

I set off down the hall.
When I looked back,
Cassie was humming along
to Dashboard Confessional.
I don't think she'd heard
the song before.
And I didn't remember
its name.
Something about
growing up fast.

Her arms were pumping.
As she put away bins of peppers.

Simple movements in space.
That held no scam at all.

And somehow I knew
that everything was beautiful and holy.

Or something like that.

Everything-everything-everything
would be alright
in the end.

BUT THAT THOUGHT PASSED QUICKLY

When I swung open
the stall,
I saw the toilet
was clogged.

With paper towels.

The water
was up to the top.

A small puddle
I needed to mop
was at the porcelain base.

Some giggling middle schoolers
had gone in there earlier.

Were kids always the same?

Now I knew what
it was like
to be on the other side.

It was like

there was a bridge

through time.

And I stood on
both ends of
that bridge.

Staring at myself.

Wondering who I was.

This was
all a trick,
wasn’t it?

Time was
the biggest scam
of all.

THAT THOUGHT ALSO PASSED

In the corner,
I could still see
the message that
Felix had scribbled
from years ago.
No one ever
removed the marker.

Our secret alphabet.
The code of our friendship.

The language of
a lost world.

I tried to call up
the hidden meaning.
To find it somewhere
in the circuits of my brain.

I didn't know
what the symbols meant
anymore.

WANT TO KEEP READING?

If you liked this book, check out another book from West 44 Books:
THE REAL UNREAL
BY RYAN WOLF

ISBN: 9781978596689

Bright
  spirals
    screaming.

NEW WORLD ORDER SCUM
shouts across
the brick
in a sharp yellow.

FREEDOM WINS
waves beside it,
a proud blue.

WE WILL NOT OBEY
has a
grim green grin.

And
in the bloodiest
drips
of hot red,
it reads:

ALL
YOU
DEVILS
WILL BE
JUDGED

The graffiti
     is flung
everywhere.

Spat
on each side
of the building.
Sneering from
the limestone walls.

Bits of
broken glass
litter
the ground.
Sprinkled
     over
the sidewalk
like shiny
balls of hail.

What is left
of the windows
looks like
a thousand
tiny
teeth.

There are small gleams
of color
among the shards.

The stained glass
was over
a hundred years old.

But
what
does
it
matter?

Whoever did this
didn't care.

The vandals even
knocked
the nose
      off
one of the
gargoyles.

I don't know how
they reached
that high.

"NATE!"

For a moment
I imagine
the call comes
from the noseless gargoyle.

ABOUT THE AUTHOR

Ryan Wolf is the author of novels for young adult and middle grade readers, as well as the *Creepy Critter Keepers* chapter book series for children. He has also published stories, poems, and nonfiction. Wolf's work has been recognized by the Junior Library Guild, Kirkus Reviews, Publishers Weekly and School Library Journal. His debut young adult novel, *Watches and Warnings*, was nominated for the North Star YA Award. Wolf holds his B.A. from Canisius College and his M.A. in the humanities from the University of Chicago. He currently resides in Buffalo, NY, with his wife and two children.